DAMIAN DROOTH
ACE DETECTIVE

DAMIAN DROOTH
ACE DETECTIVE

BARBARA MITCHELHILL

Illustrated by TONY ROSS

ANDERSEN PRESS
LONDON

First published in 2010 by
Andersen Press Limited
20 Vauxhall Bridge Road
London SW1V 2SA
www.andersenpress.co.uk
www.barbaramitchelhill.com

British Library Cataloguing in Publication Data available.

ISBN 978 184 939 097 2

Printed and bound in Great Britain by CPI Bookmarque, Croydon CR0 4TD

CONTENTS

DAMIAN DROOTH
SUPERSLEUTH

THE CASE OF
THE DISAPPEARING
DAUGHTER

Chapter 1

My name is Drooth. Damian Drooth. I track down criminals and solve crimes. A kind of one-kid, clean-up-the-world service.

How did I start? Let me tell you . . .

It was last year. The summer holidays had started and I was BORED! You know how it is when all your friends are away at the seaside or – worse still – at Disneyland.

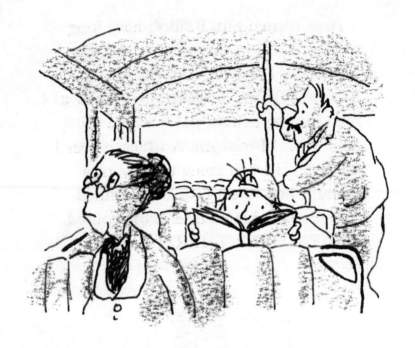

I was riding on a 39 bus at the time. I was feeling dead miserable, when I noticed a book on the seat next to me. *A Hundred Ways to Catch a Criminal*. I had nothing better to do – so I read it.

After that I was hooked! My life changed overnight. I was no longer a bored brat. A droopy drop-out. I was a supersleuth and my mission was to rid the world of crime.

As it turned out, I didn't have long to wait. I was in the supermarket that afternoon. I was heading for the Assorted Crisps Section, when I saw a man lurking behind the freezers. Suspicious! I thought. A villain if ever I saw one! If I was going to prevent a crime, I had to act fast. So I jumped on the vegetable counter and shouted, 'THIEF! OVER THERE! GET HIM!'

For a second, everybody in the supermarket stood still and stared at me. Then they rushed over to the Freezer Section. (The crook was shaking with fear by this time.) They surrounded him. Some bashed him

with their shopping baskets. Others grabbed him. He was finished, I could tell.

Me? I stayed cool and walked through the checkout. I didn't want publicity.

But that day, there was more . . .

On the way home, I saw a man snatch a bag outside a shop. He slung it into a big black Rover and drove off. A getaway car! I knew about them. I pulled out my supersleuth notebook and scribbled down the registration number. Then I dashed down the street to find a telephone.

'Excuse me!' I said to the woman in the call box. 'This is an emergency.' I grabbed the phone and dialled 999.

That was my first day as a crime buster. Pretty good, eh?

Unfortunately, Mum didn't see it that way. On Friday, she got two letters.

Dear Madam,
Please do us a favour and keep your son out of our supermarket. My store detective does not like being accused of shoplifting by a small boy. He was very embarrassed. He was only doing his job.
Yours faithfully,
P J Handy
Manager, Save-a-Lot Superstore

Dear Mrs Drooth,

No thanks to your son, I almost spent last night in jail. Please explain to him that I was putting an old lady's shopping bag into my taxi. I was not snatching it. He must be barmy to think that.

A L Fair
Ace Taxi Company

When Mum read the letters, her face turned a weird shade of purple. This happens when she gets angry (which is quite often lately). I think she should go and see a doctor.

11

Chapter 2

I have to admit, I made mistakes at
first. So I started studying dead
seriously. I wanted to be the best
private eye ever. I watched loads of
films on TV. I sat in my pyjamas in the
front room with the curtains drawn.
All day long. Black and white films.
Colour films. Films about Sherlock
Holmes . . . Miss Marple . . . Mike
Hammer . . . Inspector Morse . . . You
name 'em – I watched 'em.

Mum wasn't impressed. 'It's sunny outside,' she said. 'Why don't you play football like the other kids? It's not natural.'

It's difficult to be a supersleuth in our street. But I was determined! By the end of the week I had watched so many crimes being solved that I worked out a theory of my own!

This is my theory.

ANYONE WITH EYES SET CLOSE TOGETHER IS NOT TO BE TRUSTED AND IS UP TO NO GOOD. THEY ARE VERY PROBABLY CRIMINALS.

After that, I knew I was ready to start my career. I would go out and track down crooks . . . swindlers . . . bank robbers . . . forgers (I must remember to check my piggy bank for counterfeit coins). It was a serious task. I decided to start the next day.

Just my luck! Mum saw me slipping out of the back door in my supersleuth gear. She looked at me suspiciously. 'Just going to solve a crime, Mum,' I explained but she slammed the door shut. 'No way, Damian,' she said. 'I

want to keep my eye on you. You can forget this detective stuff. I don't want more embarrassing letters.'

This was bad news. Did James Bond ever have problems like this? Was Sherlock Holmes ever kept in by his mum? No! I felt depressed.

'You can come to work with me,' said Mum. 'That will keep you out of trouble.'

Mum runs a company called HOME COOKING UNLIMITED. She cooks for weddings and parties and stuff like that. When she takes me with her, I always get stuck with the washing up. Dead boring.

'I'm up at Harbury Hall today,' she said as we packed the van with a million bread rolls. 'There's a film crew working up there all week.'

A film crew, eh? Actors. Camera operators. Stunt artists. I began to feel quite perky.

'Don't get any funny ideas,' said Mum. 'You're doing the washing up.'

What did I tell you?

Once we were on the site, Mum carried piles of plates into the food tent. (I am never allowed to do this after a little accident I had last year. Can I help it if plates are slippery?)

I sat and ate my early morning bag
of crisps and read the newspaper. (We
detectives have to keep up-to-date.) It
was *full* of stories of unsolved crimes.
The police clearly needed help. And
here I was trapped in a food tent. What
a waste of a brilliant mind!

But things brightened up later. A
man called Victor DeVito dropped into
the tent. As it turned out, he was the
film director. A real big shot! He didn't
go anywhere without a crowd of
people taking notes and saying, 'Yes,
Victor.' 'Just as you say, Victor.'

I had never met a film director
before. But I stayed cool. I kept my

autograph book in my pocket. I'd wait till later.

'Howdee, ma'am!' he said to my mum. (He was American.) 'I just stopped by to introduce myself. You catering folk are real important on the set. Yes, sir!'

I could tell Mum was pleased. She gave one of those funny smiles and her cheeks turned pink.

'And who are you, sonny?' he said to me.

'Damian Drooth, Supersleuth,' I said. Then I whipped out the Identity Card I'd made the night before. He was dead impressed.

'Well, Damian! I can tell you that there are plenty of crooks in the film business. Watch out for 'em, will you?'

My first commission! A crime watcher on a film set. Wow! I couldn't promise to catch *every* crook but I'd do my best. From now on, I'd be on the lookout.

Chapter 3

Mr DeVito had a daughter called Trixibelle. An unusual name, you must admit. But everybody's got to be called something.

You could tell her dad was rich. She had all the gear. The trainers. The flash jacket. The personal stereo. But she was OK. She stayed behind when her dad went to check out cameras and stuff. She gave me a packet of Charley Chip's Chocolate Drops. She had loads. Personally, I prefer Smoky Bacon Crisps.

'You're so lucky, Damian,' she said as we sat eating. 'You've got a mom who cooks for you. My mom's just an actress, you know. She's never home. Right now she's in Hong Kong.'

'Acting's really interesting,' I said. But Trixibelle shook her head.

'It's not as interesting as cooking. That's what I want to do when I grow up. But Pops says I'll be too rich to be a cook.'

Being rich sounded pretty good to me. At least you didn't get stuck with the washing up.

Somebody was calling her name outside the tent.

'That'll be my new tutor, Miss Berry,' she sighed. 'I'll have to go.'

I was amazed. I'd never met anyone with a personal tutor. But then I'd never met anyone as rich as the DeVito family.

Trixibelle walked away from the tent. Her tutor was waiting by the large white caravan opposite. Wow!

Was that really a teacher? She looked like a film star! She was tall with long blonde hair and red lipstick. And she wore really cool shades, too. She was nothing like Mr Grimethorpe, our class teacher. Lucky old Trixibelle!

By half past ten there was a long queue outside the food tent. Hungry actors. Ravenous technicians. All wanting Mum's coffee and cakes. Me? I was soon up to my elbows in greasy water. I ask you! After an hour and a half, my hands had turned ghostly white and as wrinkled as prunes.

'If you can't do it faster than that, Damian, we'll never be ready for lunch,' Mum moaned.

I admit I wasn't the fastest washer-up in the world. It was hard keeping my mind on dirty plates. Luckily, I was saved from total boredom when one of the security guards stuck his head into the tent.

'Anybody seen Trixibelle?' he asked.

I lifted my hands out of the water. 'She's in the caravan over there,' I said, pointing across the grass.

The guard shook his head. 'Not for half an hour,' he said. 'Her tutor reported her missing. Miss Berry went out to get a cup of coffee and when she got back, Trixibelle had gone.'

'I'll find her,' I said, drying my hands on a tea towel. 'I'm brilliant at tracking down missing persons.' This was not strictly true. But it was a great excuse to get away from the washing up.

Mum wasn't keen. Her lips were
pressed tight together. 'He's got work
to do,' she said.

The guard looked daggers. 'Mr
DeVito will be very angry if we lose his
daughter,' he said in a threatening kind
of way. 'Your son would be a great
help.'

So Mum let me go.

That was how the Case of the
Disappearing Daughter began.

Chapter 4

I wasn't really worried about
Trixibelle. In my opinion, she had
slipped off somewhere to get away
from lessons. I knew all about that. I'd
done it myself. Particularly during
spelling tests.

I followed the guard across the
grass. Miss Berry was standing by the
caravan. She had a large tissue clasped
to her nose and she was sniffing. I
could tell she was upset.

'Try not to worry, Miss Berry,' I said. 'I'll get her back for you. You can rely on me.'

She gave me a wonderful smile and a tingle ran from the top of my head down to my toes. I felt like a knight on a crusade.

It seemed that everyone was out searching for Trixibelle. (Except Mum who was doing the washing up.) The whole crew had stopped work to look. I used all my detective's experience – but still I found nothing. Not a single clue.

Suddenly, Victor DeVito came rushing out of his caravan (the biggest on the site) and climbed onto the roof. Was the man crazy or what?

'Listen, people!' he shouted through his megaphone.

Everything went deathly quiet.

'I have some terrible news. My Trixibelle has been kidnapped!'

There were gasps of oohs and aaahs. Nobody could believe it.

'It's true!' the director continued, holding his hand up for silence. (Mr Grimethorpe, our class teacher, often does this.) 'I just got a phone call and some crazy people are demanding a million pounds for my baby.'

He took a large handkerchief and blew his nose.

'I'll pay it if I have to – but in the meantime, the police are doing their best to find out where she is.'

Now I know for a fact that the police often miss clues that are right under their noses. So I decided that somehow, I would have to track down the criminals. After all, Victor DeVito himself had asked me to be on the lookout for crooks. It was the least I could do.

Chapter 5

I hurried back to tell Mum about the kidnapping.

'I've heard,' she said. 'Miss Berry is very upset. She's gone to lie down.'

Poor Miss Berry! I thought. She must be feeling dead guilty. Letting Mr DeVito's daughter slip away.

'I think I'll take her a cup of tea,' I said. 'She'll like that.' This was a good chance to impress Miss Berry with my supersleuth ideas for finding Trixibelle.

'That's thoughtful of you, Damian,' said Mum. I could tell she was surprised.

I was careful not to spill the tea as I pushed open the caravan door. I suppose I should have knocked – but I didn't. What I saw shocked me, I can tell you. Miss Berry wasn't lying down at all. She was bending over, stuffing clothes into a suitcase.

I scanned the caravan with my detective laser vision. On a table were a pair of shades and a long blonde wig. I gasped. That was when Miss Berry whizzed round. What a shock! She wasn't blonde after all. She had short dark hair.

'Oh dear!' she said, grabbing hold of
her wig. 'What a mess I look, Damian!
I . . . I was just keeping myself busy.
Just tidying up.' She slammed the
suitcase shut and took the cup and
saucer. 'How very kind of you, dear
boy. Poor, poor Trixibelle.'

She smiled but she couldn't win me
over. Things had changed. Now I
could see that her eyes were set very
close together. If my theory was right,
Miss Berry was a criminal in disguise.

Chapter 6

After that, I decided to keep an eye on
the caravan. This was difficult as Mum
insisted I finished the washing up. I
had to keep looking over my shoulder.
My neck got terrible cramp. It was
agony.

Nothing happened for a bit. Then Mum asked me to take the rubbish out. What a piece of luck! Just as I left the tent, I saw Miss Berry sneaking out of the caravan. She was carrying a suitcase! I dumped the rubbish sack and followed her – keeping my distance just like detectives do.

Before long, I realised that she was
heading for the car park. So she had a
car! She could be away in no time.
Then my prime suspect would be lost
for ever.

She stopped by a large red Ford and
took some keys from her handbag. I
dropped down between two vans and

watched over the bonnet. My heart was pounding like a rock band. She was going to escape. How could I stop her?

As she opened the door, a voice shouted, 'Hey you! Wait!'

Miss Berry spun round. A security
guard was hurrying towards her.

'You're not thinking of leaving the
site, are you, miss?'

Her piggy eyes nearly popped out of
her head. I could see she was shaking.

'Just going for a little ride,' she said,
cool as you like.

'Mr DeVito said *nobody* should leave,' said the guard, who was pretty scary.

But Miss Berry smiled and walked round the car. 'I'm so upset, officer. Trixibelle is my dear little pupil, you see.' You could tell the guard was taken in by her film star looks. She stood there telling him loads of lies. And he believed her! It was clear he wasn't well trained in detective work.

I didn't waste any time. While they were talking on one side of the car, I crept around the other side. Slowly, I opened the back door. I slipped in and I lay on the floor behind the driver's seat. Wherever Miss Berry was going, so was I!

Chapter 7

Miss Berry drove like a maniac. She whizzed round bends. She tore down hills. I felt sick, I can tell you. When I heard her dialling on the car phone, I couldn't believe it! It was crazy! She couldn't drive with two hands – never mind one!

'Zac! It's me,' she said. 'I'm on my way. Are you ready to move the girl? DeVito should come up with the money within the next hour.'

So my theory of close-set eyes was
right. Miss Berry was a criminal. A
kidnapper, no less! I was on her track.
All I had to do was to get Trixibelle
out of her clutches.

When she screeched to a halt, my
head smashed against the back of the
seat. SPLAT! I lay there. My brain was
spinning. I heard the car door open
and then Miss Berry walked away.
Somehow, I had to get up!

I was seeing stars but I pulled myself
together. I peeped out of the window.
We had stopped in a deserted
farmyard – but there was no sign of
Miss Berry. Just loads of barns and
derelict sheds. It was a perfect hiding
place. Nobody would come to a place
like this.

The problem was – where to start looking. Trixibelle could be anywhere.

I opened the car door and slid onto the ground. Like a marine on a combat mission, I crabbed my way across the farmyard. Except for the noise of swallows twittering, there wasn't a sound. No voice. Nothing.

I stood up. I pressed my back to the
wall and hoped Miss Berry wasn't
looking out of one of the windows. My
forehead was sticky with sweat (or was
it blood?).

I raced across to a large barn. I
stopped and stood panting by a

doorway. That was when my luck changed. I glanced down and saw a trail of chocolate drops. They were Charley Chip's Chocolate Drops. I could spot them a mile off. Trixibelle had left a clue! Good thinking!

I felt hopeful. I walked through the door of the barn and climbed some stone steps. It was dark inside and I had to feel my way. Luckily, the chocolate drops went right to the top.

They led to a wooden door and I pressed my ear against it. Voices! That guy called Zac and Miss Berry!

I panicked. Well, who wouldn't? I needed help. I had to run.

I was about to turn and go back when the worst thing possible happened. The door opened.

'You!' said Miss Berry.

'Who's he?' yelled the man. (This was Zac.)

Miss Berry leaned forward to grab me.

I stepped backward.

Miss Berry slipped.

Zac tripped over her.

Smash! They crashed down the stairs. Bang! Clunk! Boing!

They even pulled some bales of hay on top of them. There they lay, moaning. Only their feet and arms visible. What a sight!

Trixibelle was in the room upstairs, bound and gagged. No problem! I had

her free in a flash.

'You're wonderful, Damian,' she said. She flung her arms round my neck and gave me a sloppy kiss.

I was dead embarrassed. 'Don't mention it,' I said. 'It was nothing.'

We raced downstairs where the two
kidnappers were lying moaning under
the bales. Their arms were flailing
about – but they couldn't move.

'Sit on 'em,' I said. 'That way they
can't get away.'

Trixi sat on her tutor. I sat on Zac.
The problem was, what to do next? If
one of us went for help, one of the
kidnappers could get free. But we
couldn't stay there for ever. My brain

was pounding, trying to find a
solution. What would Sherlock Holmes
do? What would James Bond do? What
would Superman do?

'We could always use my mobile,'
said Trixibelle.

I was gobsmacked! She fished a
phone out of her pocket and dialled
999. She was smarter than I thought.

Chapter 8

In no time the barn was surrounded. Five police cars – not to mention the Range Rovers bringing Victor DeVito and the entire film crew.

'We're here, babe!' shouted Mr DeVito through his megaphone. 'Your daddy's come to get you.'

Miss Berry and Zac were soon locked up in a police cell. We went back to Harbury Hall and Victor DeVito threw a fantastic party. There was mountains of food and I didn't have to wash up.

'I'm proud of you, Damian,' said Trixi's dad.

My mum nodded and wiped a tear from her eye.

'You saved my baby, sonny,' said Victor. 'Thank you sincerely.'

It was all a bit embarrassing. 'It's the training that does it,' I explained. 'I'm a well-known supersleuth in my home town. It was all in a day's work.'

Victor nodded as if he understood. I could tell he was dead impressed.

Afterwards the police inspector came to talk to me. I think he wanted to pick up some tips on solving crimes.

'A real detective looks for clues,' I said.

He pulled his notebook out ready to

jot down my ideas.

'And what clues made you suspect these two?'

I smiled. 'It's all a question of experience,' I said. I didn't mention my theory of close-set eyes. That's my little secret! They don't call me Supersleuth for nothing.

DAMIAN DROOTH
SUPERSLEUTH

THE CASE OF
THE POP STAR'S
WEDDING

*For Tom who likes football
and Alexandra who loves pink* (B.M.)

Chapter 1

My name is Drooth. Damian Drooth. Crime buster extraordinary. Ace detective.

Let me tell you about my latest case.

It started when a letter arrived for Mum. It was addressed to Mrs Drooth, Home Cooking Unlimited.

'Guess who this is from!' she shrieked. I could tell she was in a real tizz.

So I read the letter.

Dear Mrs Drooth,
I was wondering if you would be
interested in providing the food for my
wedding. Perhaps you could come to see
me and discuss the menu.
                    Yours sincerely,
                    Tiger Lilly

I stared at the signature. I was
gobsmacked.

'***Tiger Lilly?***' I yelled. (It was
difficult to stay calm.) '***The singer?***
One of the Bay Babes?'

Mum nodded and my head
exploded. She was my most favourite
singer EVER! I was her NUMERO
UNO fan! Wow! Wow! Wow!

That morning, Mum telephoned
Tiger Lilly and arranged a meeting.

'I'll come with you,' I said.

'I don't think so,' said Mum as she
wrote the date in her diary.

'You might get lost,' I insisted.

'I can read a map, Damian.'

'I could be your secretary and take notes.'

'I don't want a secretary.'

I tried a different approach.

'Right! I'll go on hunger strike if you don't take me!'

Mum sighed. 'Don't be stupid, Damian!' she said. 'NO!'

In the end, she gave in. My mum's brain power is no match for my razor-sharp cunning.

And so I got to meet the fabulous Tiger Lilly.

Chapter 2

Tiger Lilly's place was mega huge!
Even the drive was longer than our
street. As we pulled up outside the
front door, there she was waiting for us
on the steps. A Star! Some guys would
have gone wild. But not me! Fame
doesn't bother me. Even though her
eyes were deep blue and her hair was
blonde and right down to her waist – I
stayed cool.

Then Mum spoke.

'This is my little boy, Damian,' she said in her mumsy voice. 'I hope you don't mind him coming with me. There was no one to look after him – and he's inclined to get into trouble.'

I ask you! Embarrassing or what? But I stuffed my hands in my pockets and just said, 'Hi!' as if I met celebrities every day.

We followed Tiger Lilly down the hall and into a fantastic room with big comfy chairs and a dangly chandelier.

'Well, Damian,' she said, as she poured us some tea. 'I've got a little brother and he's always in trouble, too!'

'It may seem like trouble to some,' I said, darkly. 'But the fact is I work undercover. I'm a Private Eye.'

I could see she was dead impressed.

'I track down crooks . . . bank robbers . . . forgers . . . that kind of thing.'

Tiger Lilly turned and looked at Mum.

'You didn't tell me you'd got your own detective agency, Mrs Drooth!' she said. Then she winked – or maybe she had something in her eye. 'He'll be useful on the day of the wedding. Don't want any of my presents getting stolen, eh?'

Mum looked horrified. 'Oh, Damian won't be here on your wedding day,' she said. 'I wouldn't want him here with all your guests around. He'll just get in the way.'

Cheek! After all the times I've helped out! Only a few breakages. Only a few mistakes. That's understandable, isn't it?

Luckily, Tiger Lilly *insisted* I went.
'You organise the food, Mrs Drooth,
and Damian can keep a lookout for
suspicious characters.'

Mum couldn't say anything, could
she? I had been employed as a private
detective at the Wedding-of-the-Year.

Chapter 3

There were three weeks to go before the wedding and I had to be on top form. I needed to sharpen up my sleuthing skills. In my Supersleuth Notebook, I had a theory of detection to help me in my work: ANYONE WITH EYES SET CLOSE TOGETHER IS NOT TO BE TRUSTED.

(This was very useful in my first case – known for miles around as The Case of the Disappearing Daughter.)

But one theory wasn't enough. After all, I could be up against hardened criminals at the wedding. I decided to spend the time studying detective stories. There were some great ones in my comics. Mum didn't understand, of course.

'Why not read a proper book?' she said. But I stuck to it regardless.

After ten days of serious study, I came up with:
ANYONE WITH A BEARD (PARTICULARLY A DARK ONE) IS PROBABLY UP TO NO GOOD.

Working out a theory is one thing. Proving it is another. This is how I did it. *(For those who want to pick up hints about detective work, I've copied out my notebook in my best handwriting.)*

MONDAY

Our teacher, Mr Grimethorpe is off sick. They say it's stress. But how can that be? Teachers have it dead easy! If you ask me, he spends too much time shouting and thumping his desk.

Our new teacher is Mr Symes <u>WHO HAS A BEARD</u>.

<u>TUESDAY</u>
Mr Symes is dead keen on money.
He counts dinner money twice.
He needs watching.

<u>WEDNESDAY</u>
9.15 MS counts trip
money 3 times!!!!!!
9.30 MS puts money in
his briefcase.
THIS PROVES HE IS A
THIEF.

9.35 Work out cunning plan in back of maths book.

9.45 Put plan into action. Stuff briefcase under my jumper. Creep out of classroom when MS isn't looking. Go to find Mrs Frank our school secretary.

10.0 School office locked. No sign of Mrs Frank. Probably making tea and chocolate biscuits for the Head.

10.10 Hide briefcase in cloakroom. Will pick it up later.

10.15 Go back to class.

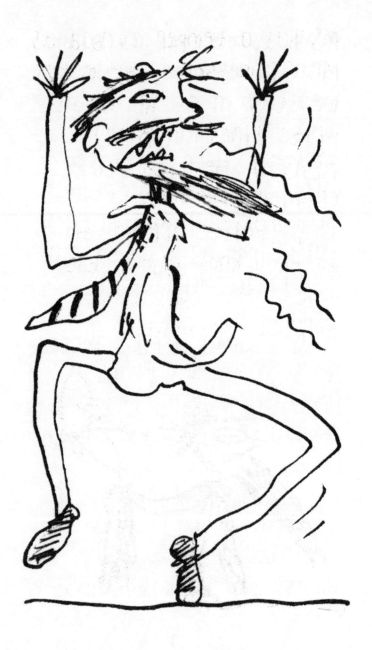

MS has a temper as bad as Mr Grimethorpe. He makes me stay in at break and write lines. FOR NO REASON. He is a real criminal for sure.
11.0 Police arrive. How do they know about the money? MS looks dead worried. No wonder!

THURSDAY

9.0 No sign of Mr Symes. I expect he's in prison.
I will not mention my part in his downfall to the police.

So my Theory of the Beard was proved. Now I could track down the craftiest criminal who dared to go to Tiger Lilly's wedding.

Chapter 4

On the morning of the wedding, Mum was in a real flap. Me? I'd got my gear together, my notepad and my pen – and I was ready to take on the big names of the underworld, if necessary.

'Damian!' Mum shouted. 'Don't stand there in a daze. Help me get these puddings into the van.'

I ask you! Does James Bond carry puddings for his mum? No! But that day, she was in a bit of a mood. So I did it. I picked up a big chocolate mousse and carried it as carefully as I could. Was it my fault if the path was uneven? Was it my fault if I slipped?

Mum didn't speak to me all the way to Tiger Lilly's place. She just gripped the wheel and frowned at the road ahead. She was in a real mood.

When we reached the house, there was a security man on the gate. He was huge and wore a badge with DEAN on it. I must say, I was surprised that Tiger Lilly had employed him when she knew I was coming.

Mum stopped and wound down the window.

'Catering,' she said.

'I need to see your passes,' said Dean.

Mum handed her card out of the window. I leaned over and flashed the detective badge I had made the night before. We were waved straight in. No problem.

The lawn in front of Tiger Lilly's
house was filled with an enormous tent
(called a *marquee*). And there were
loads of people milling around,
carrying chairs and arranging flowers.
Mum parked the van behind the
marquee and started unloading the

food. She was dashing backwards and
forwards like a wild thing carrying
trays and dishes and got really out of
breath. If you ask me, she's not at all
fit. She could do with a good work-out
at the gym.

I offered to help but she wasn't keen. She said she'd rather do it herself.

'All right,' I said. 'I'll go and look round the grounds for crooks and that.'

Mum gave me one of her looks. 'You dare get into trouble!' she shouted over a pile of vol-au-vents. 'I've got enough to think about without worrying about you.'

'Stay cool!' I said. 'I'm in control.'

Mum's face turned scarlet. Probably her blood pressure. It's best to ignore it. So I put on my shades and walked away.

It wasn't long before I saw a man who was dead suspicious. He was wearing a black suit with a white shirt and was carrying a black leather case.

Spooky! And – guess what? His eyes were really close together. (Detection Theory number 1.) If that wasn't enough – he had a BLACK BEARD, too! (Detection Theory number 2.) I had hit the jackpot! This man was a mega criminal.

I did a quick sketch and made some notes in my Supersleuth Notebook. Then I followed him into the house. It was obvious he was planning to steal the wedding presents.

Chapter 5

I walked behind him with my back
pressed against the wall. Just like
detectives on TV. But before I got
close, somebody shouted, 'Hey, kid!'
and a security guard grabbed me by
the collar.

'What do you think you're doing in
here, eh?'

I checked his badge (which said
CURT) and showed him mine.

'I'm with Mum's catering company,'
I said.

Curt grunted.

'I'm Tiger Lilly's personal protection officer.'

Curt laughed! What was so funny?

'Out you go, sonny,' he said, as if I was a kid. 'Go and find your mum.'

Of course, I did no such thing. I owed it to Tiger Lilly to watch over her presents. I walked away, pretending to head for the marquee. When I was sure that Curt had gone, I hurried back towards the house and sneaked down the side.

As I peeped in through a window, I
saw the presents spread out on a table.
Each one had a label showing who had
sent it. There were masses of silver
plates and goblets – stuff like that.
There were old paintings, too, that
must have been worth a bomb. But in
the middle of it all was a fantastic
diamond necklace. A large label said,
'To Tiger Lily on our wedding day
from Gary with love and kisses.' YUK!

Tiger Lilly was marrying Gary Blaze. I didn't know why. He was a football player with skinny legs and no hair. He was useless at everything except scoring goals. Why did Tiger Lilly fall for someone like that, I ask you? She needed a guy with laser brainpower. Someone who could spot a thug a mile away.

As I looked through the window, the
man with the beard walked into the
room. He stood and stared at the
diamond necklace. It was obvious that
he was going to nick it when the not-
very-bright security guard (CURT)
wasn't looking.

I worked out a plan. I ran round to
the front door, hid behind the ivy and
waited. Ten minutes later the man in
black came out and I followed him
down the path. Halfway, he stopped,
looked at his watch and started
running towards the marquee.
Suspicious or what? But I was onto
him.

By that time, the reception was in full swing. The crook went round the back of the tent, lifted a loose flap and sneaked in. He was cunning all right! But he wasn't going to get away.

I hurried to the main entrance of the tent. Inside, everybody was eating and talking. I could see Tiger Lilly looking fantastic in a long white dress with flowers in her hair and silver nail varnish. Gary Blaze looked stupid in a blue suit. (What did she see in him?)

I looked round trying to spot the
thief. YES! There he was. Hiding
amongst the band. Pretending to play
a saxophone. Very clever, I don't
think.

If he thought he would get away
with the necklace – he was making a
big mistake!

Chapter 6

I had to tell Tiger Lilly what was going on. I knew she'd be dead impressed when she heard I'd saved her diamond necklace. I started running towards her but, before I could get near, a hand landed on my shoulder and a security guard (KELVIN) pulled me up sharp.

I yelled. But nobody came to help. They were too busy stuffing themselves with Mum's food (chicken and all the trimmings).

'What do you think you're playing at?' said Kelvin as he dragged me outside.

I started to explain. 'I'm tracking down . . .'

But before I could finish, Curt came dashing out of the big house shouting, 'Come quick, Kelvin! Quick!'

Kelvin dropped me like a hot potato and ran. I followed, of course.

Something was up!

'The diamond necklace has been nicked,' said Curt.

'I know that,' I said – just to be helpful.

The guards turned and looked at me.

'How do you know?' said Kelvin.

'I'm a Private Eye,' I said, holding out my badge.

They raised their eyebrows and smirked. But I ignored them.

'I was watching the presents when I saw someone take the necklace.'

(It was *nearly* true. I *almost* saw him. It couldn't have been anyone else, could it?)

I flicked open my Supersleuth Notebook.

'The thief was a tall, thin male with a beard, wearing a black suit, a white shirt and carrying a black case.'

They looked at me as if I'd crawled out from under a stone.

'Stupid boy!' said Curt. 'That's Dave. He plays in the band!'

I smiled, knowingly. 'Just a cover for his criminal activities,' I said. 'I reckon the necklace is in the case.'

They snorted and pushed me to one side.

'Ring the police, Curt,' said Kelvin. 'Don't tell any of the guests or the wedding will be ruined.'

Curt got out his mobile and dialled 999.

'As for you!' said Kelvin, turning to me. 'I thought we'd sent you back to your mother.'

He didn't let me explain. He slung me over his shoulders like a sack of carrots. Cheek!

I thought he'd take me to the refreshment tent. But he didn't. He took me to the van.

'Right!' he said, swinging open the back door. 'You can stay there until your mum's finished with the food. Then *she* can look after you.' He flung me inside and slammed the door shut.

I didn't have the energy to try to escape. Suddenly I felt weak. My blood sugar was dropping. My brain was slowing down. I knew it was the stress of chasing criminals – and lack of food. Luckily, I had spotted a chocolate gateau in the back of the van. It's one of my favourites. So I had a slice, in the interest of successful crime detection.

(REMEMBER THIS TIP: Chocolate gateau is excellent for energy.)

I felt so much better after one slice that I had another. The more I ate, the more my brainpower increased. It was amazing! Of course, I hid the plate so Mum wouldn't notice the missing gateau. I didn't want her getting upset.

Now I was ready for action.
Escaping would be no problem. The
lock on the van door was broken, see.
When Mum locked it up at night, she
had to put a chain round the handles.
She said it was cheaper than having a
new lock fitted. But the guard didn't
know that, did he? He thought he'd
locked me in. Tee hee!

Slowly, I opened the door and
peeped out. I was a few metres from

the entrance of the marquee. I could see Tiger Lilly (still looking gorgeous) and the band on the far side. But there were security guards everywhere. It was almost impossible to get in without being seen. So how could I reach the thief and save the diamond necklace?

Chapter 7

Being a trained detective, I soon had the problem sorted.

Between the van and the entrance was a large trolley with the wedding cake on top. Perfect! All I had to do was distract the waiter who was standing nearby. (He was wrinkled and stooping – at least forty.) Then I would hide under the trolley.

'Excuse me!' I said, climbing out of the van. 'Somebody's looking for you. I can hear them shouting over there.'

The waiter looked puzzled but went off round the back of the van. That was my chance. I dashed across, lifted the cloth and slipped onto the bottom layer of the trolley.

The waiter was back in no time.

'Huh! Young 'uns,' I heard him mutter. 'Up to their tricks!'

Then he pushed the trolley into the marquee, across the wooden floor and stopped in front of the bride's table. Everybody cheered and clapped as Tiger Lilly and the bald footballer walked towards it to cut the cake.

That's when I leapt out.

'HOLD EVERYTHING!' I shouted. (I had heard a detective say this in a film. I thought it sounded good.)

'STAND CLEAR!' I added, just for good measure. 'THERE IS A CROOK IN HERE AND HE'S STOLEN A DIAMOND NECKLACE!'

I must admit, I was surprised Tiger Lilly didn't rush to my side. Hadn't she understood what I'd said?

Instead, security guards were running towards me from every corner of the tent like crazy gorillas.

I jumped back onto the trolley and, pushing off with one foot, I skimmed over the floor towards the band.

'IT'S HIM!' I shouted. 'THE ONE WITH THE SAXOPHONE! HE STOLE THE NECKLACE AND IT'S IN HIS BLACK CASE!'

At this point, the trolley ran out of control and smashed into the band. I whizzed through the air like Superman and landed on the stage while the cake shot across the floor leaving behind a lake of white icing and cream.

I stared up into the face of the crook. (His beard looked even worse close up.)

'GOTCHA!' I said.

But it was the man *behind* him who
suddenly leapt off the stage and made
a run for it. Unluckily for him, he
skidded on the splodge of cream. His
feet flew out from under him and he
crashed onto his back like a beached
whale.

Meanwhile, I clambered across the
stage and reached in his case.

'I think he's forgotten something,' I
called out and held up the necklace for
all to see. Now everybody was on their
feet. They stood in a great circle round
the crook, pushing and shoving to get
a better look.

All this excitement – and then the police arrived.

'What's going on?' said the Inspector. 'Have you caught the thief?'

'Thanks to this boy, we have,' said Tiger Lilly. 'This is Damian Drooth and he could teach the police a thing or two about solving crimes.'

As she spoke, she put her arm round my shoulder. I almost fainted with pride.

Chapter 8

I expect you're wondering how I managed to track down the jewel thief. After all, he didn't have a beard like my first suspect.

Well, I must admit there was a bit of a mistake. You see, I'm not brilliant at names of instruments and stuff. So when I shouted, 'It's the one with the saxophone!' I got it wrong. I should have said a trumpet.

For your information, this is a
trumpet . . .

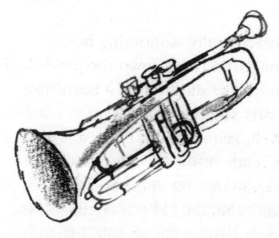

this is a saxophone.

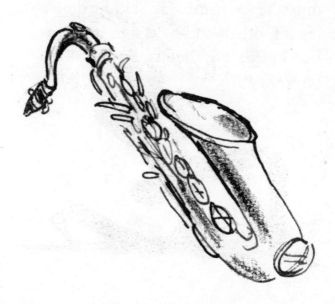

But it didn't matter. As it turned out, the man who stole the necklace *really was* playing the saxophone. Lucky mistake, eh?

As for Tiger Lilly, she was thrilled I'd foiled the crook. I asked her if she'd sign my CDs and she said, 'Oh Damian, I'll give you a copy of every CD I've ever made **and** sign it for you.' Then she kissed me on the cheek. That was a bit girlie for me but it was OK, really.

Gary Blaze went all smarmy and said, 'Thanks ever so much, Damian.' I think he's a wimp. He said he'd give me a football and he'd sign it for me. But I said, 'No thanks. I'm not keen on football.'

Everybody cheered me and they
made a great fuss. They asked me what
I would like to eat and made me sit at
one of the posh tables.

'Sorry, Damian,' said Kelvin when
he brought me two plates of food.
'We've run out of chocolate gateau.
Will strawberries do?'

It's the thought that counts.

When everything had calmed down and most of the police had gone, Inspector Crockitt came over to talk to me. I'd met him before. He tries to pick up tips on solving crimes.

'How did you catch him, Damian?' he asked.

I'm too modest to tell a police inspector how to do his job. But I like to help.

'I've got this theory about beards,' I said.

'Is that how you solved this case?' he asked.

I could see he was keen to know. 'Maybe,' I said, winking at him. 'But maybe I got lucky.'

They don't call me Supersleuth for nothing.

DAMIAN DROOTH
SUPERSLEUTH

HOW TO BE
A DETECTIVE

For Louise, Lucy, Max, Tom and Felix –
also for Isabel (who especially likes notes
on Criminal Types)

Chapter 1

My name is Damian Drooth and I'm a mega successful detective. You might have heard of me. I've solved loads of crimes in our town.

Not long ago, I decided that there must be masses of kids who wanted to learn to be crime busters like me. So I put a sign in the school playground that read:

DAMIAN DROOTH, FAMOUS DETECTIVE AND SUPERSLEUTH WILL GIVE A TALK ON HOW TO SPOT CROOKS AND THIEVES AND CRIMINALS ON THE STREETS.
COME TO THE SHED AT THE BOTTOM OF THE GARDEN AT 10 O'CLOCK ON SATURDAY MORNING.
WEAR SHADES.
DO NOT BE LATE.

Entrance fee: 1 packet of crisps.

I chose Saturday because Mum was working that day. She has a business called Home Cooking Unlimited. She makes cakes and sandwiches and takes them to weddings and things. She likes to keep busy. I think she gets bored just hanging around the house.

Sometimes I go along and help her – but I didn't want to go this time. She was doing the food at a flower show. (I'm not keen on flowers.)

'I'll stay and do my homework,' I said. 'I've got this really interesting essay to do for history.'

I noticed Mum tightened her lips and screwed up her eyes. I call this her Suspicious Look.

'That doesn't sound like you, Damian,' she said. 'What are you up to?'

I didn't say anything. I just stood there looking hurt. But it did the trick.

In the end, she said, 'All right, then. But you have to stay in the house. I'll ask Mrs Robertson next door to pop round and keep an eye on you.'

Of course I agreed. If I hadn't, I would have spent Saturday at the flower show washing up and listening to people talk about fertilisers and greenfly.

Chapter 2

On Saturday morning, Mum was late loading the van. I'd almost finished my breakfast and she was still flashing in and out of the kitchen. In a rush as usual.

'Carry something out for me, will you, Damian?' she panted (showing how unfit she is).

'OK,' I said. I put down my toast and picked up a chocolate gateau. My favourite.

'No, not that,' said Mum and
grabbed it off me. 'Carry the cutlery.'

So I did. But even this didn't please
her. I know I dropped the box but
nothing was broken and I picked up
every last knife and fork. Except the
ones that fell down the drain.

In the end, she drove off at nine
o'clock which was great timing

because the kids arrived soon after for
the Detective School. They formed a
long line outside the garden shed. It
was obvious they were dead keen to
learn.

Tod Browning and his sister,
Lavender, were at the front of the
queue. So they got the seats. 'The early
detective catches the worm,' I always
say (or something like that).

I collected the entrance fees (7 bags of crisps in all) which I stashed away in a box before standing on a bucket ready to give my first talk.

'Right,' I said. 'I want to check that you've got your notebooks and pencils. Every good detective should have one.' They had.

Now I needed to impress them. I didn't say a thing. I just got out my press cuttings from the local paper.

DAMIAN DROOTH SAVES DIRECTOR'S DAUGHTER

Police were astonished when a young boy, Damian Drooth, saved the young daughter of a film director kidnapped by an international crook.

DAMIAN DROOTH FINDS STOLEN DIAMONDS

A diamond necklace belonging to a pop star was recovered by a local boy detective. Damian Drooth was guarding presents worth thousands of pounds at the wedding of Pop Star, Tiger Lily, to footballer, Gary Blaze.

I could see they were gobsmacked. Then they started asking questions.

'Don't the police get mad because you're cleverer than they are?'

'Did any crooks pay you big money to stop you telling on them?'

That kind of thing.

Lavender Browning, who was only a small kid, asked me, 'Whath's it like to be famouth, Damian?'

'Yeah, go on. Tell us,' the rest shouted.

But I was too modest to answer. Instead, I began to explain my Theories of Criminal Detection. After all, they were here to learn.

'These are the most common types of crooks you're likely to spot,' I said and I pinned two posters (drawn by me) on the wall.

CRIMINAL TYPE NO. 1
EYES SET CLOSE TOGETHER
(A good example is Mr Forrester in Class 5.
Watch out for him in future.)

CRIMINAL TYPE NO. 2
ANYBODY WITH A BEARD
(usually men)
BLACK BEARDS ARE THE WORST.
(Take a look at the new crossing
attendant.
He could be up to no good. Only time
will tell.)

Some of them were scribbling like mad in their notebooks. Some of them were yawning with the exhaustion of listening and learning. I feel just like that in Mr Johnson's maths class.

'Always remember,' I said, 'the best way to learn how to track down criminals is to be alert.'

'How do we do that, Damian?'
Harry Houseman called out.

I explained. 'If we went down to the
High Street and stayed alert, we'd
probably spot a criminal.'

'In our High Street?'

'Absolutely,' I said.

'Then let's do it!' said Tod.

I shook my head. 'Not today.'

The fact was, I was secretly looking
forward to eating the crisps before
Mum came back. Anyway, I'd
promised to stay in and I always keep
my promises. Almost always.

'Come on, Damian,' shouted
Winston Hunt. 'What are you scared
of?'

'Yeah!' called out one of the girls.
'Show us how it's done – if you can.'

Then everybody joined in. There
was nearly a riot. They were so keen.
How could I refuse? So we set off.

Chapter 3

'Just remember what I told you,' I said
when we'd reached the High Street.
'Look out for the most common types
of crooks. Check your notes, if you
need to.'

We were just passing the Post Office
when Lavender tugged at my sleeve.

'Over there, Damian. Look! A
cwiminal!'

A man with a beard was riding one
of those buggy things along the
pavement. His beard was white, so he
wasn't a major criminal. But I didn't
like to point this out.

'Mmm,' I said. 'Maybe he is . . . Or maybe not.'

But Lavender, who got easily excited, was absolutely convinced. 'He'th a wobber. He'th going to mug thomebody and take their money. I can tell.'

'OK. OK,' I said. 'I'll show you how to keep a close watch on him. Follow me.'

I pressed my back up against the wall, my cap pulled down over my eyes. All the other kids did the same. We kept our eyes fixed on the suspect as he came down the High Street. Then – just as Lavender had thought – he started heading towards a woman who was collecting for charity. And the tin was **full of money!**

'He'th going to thteal it,' said Lavender. 'What can we do?'

Harry Houseman, the biggest boy in our class, couldn't wait to be in on the action. 'Right, Lavender! I'll stop him!'

He darted forward between the buggy and the collector. He stopped, held his hand in the air and shouted, 'Don't come any closer!'

The man in the buggy-thing looked shocked. He tried to swerve to avoid Harry – or maybe he was making a getaway. I don't know which. Whatever his plans were, they were foiled. The

buggy-thing tipped over and the man went sprawling on the pavement. So he never got his hands on the collecting tin. Seconds later, there were loads of people round him. He had no chance of getting away.

Another job well done.

'Come on,' I called to Harry. 'Never stay on the scene of the crime once you've solved it.'

Chapter 4

Things were going well and I had a brilliant idea.

'I want to try out a new theory,' I said. 'You can all come with me if you like.'

'Oh yeth, Damian,' said Lavender. 'Where are we going?'

'The library,' I said. 'We can do some people-watching without anybody noticing us.'

The theory I was working on was this: people with thin lips were inclined to be crooks. Stealing jewels. Breaking into banks. That kind of thing. I worked this out from looking at the photos in the local paper. Going into the library would give me the chance to see if my theory was true.

So we walked in, took some books off the shelves and sat at the tables. Of course, everybody thought we were reading – but we weren't. We were peering over the top of the books, looking for criminal types.

We watched for at least ten minutes and then Lavender hissed, 'Pssst!' She was trying to attract my attention.

She was nodding in the direction of the librarian's desk where a large woman with a fur coat and frothy blonde hair was taking out a book. 'I think thee's one,' she whispered.

I got up and sidled over to the desk, hoping no one would notice. The other kids followed. When I got near, I could see that the woman was borrowing a suspicious book called *Loot*. (A technical term for stolen goods known only to experienced detectives.)

This was not the only suspicious thing. The woman's eyes were close together, cunningly hidden by glasses. **But best of all** – her lips were thin and tight and there were little wrinkles

round them. Bingo! She was an
excellent example of all my Criminal
Types (except she didn't have a
beard).

I turned to Lavender and gave her a
thumbs-up. The kid might make a
brilliant detective – one day.

Unfortunately, we were getting
funny looks from Miss Travis, the
librarian. I don't know why. She is
usually very understanding. She must
have had a headache or something.

The blonde woman put the book in
her bag, ready to go. As she turned
and headed for the door, I gave a
signal for the others to follow. But at
this point, my luck changed.

'Damian!' Miss Travis called. 'Please will you and your friends put away those books before you leave?'

I gritted my teeth and gave her one of my best smiles.

'We'll do it later,' I said. 'We've just got to . . .'

'NOW!' she shouted. Miss Travis never shouts. She was clearly not feeling well.

We rushed over to the table, stuck the books back on the shelves and dashed out of the library. The High Street was crowded with shoppers. Had I lost the thin-lipped woman forever? I wondered.

'She's there!' said Harry, who was so tall he could see over people's heads. 'She's level with that white van.'

Luckily she stood out from the crowd (what with her big blonde hair and her fur coat and that). We all raced after her down the High Street, which was not easy as people kept crashing into us.

'Keep your eyes fixed on her,' I panted. 'We need to know what she's up to.'

But before we could catch her, she turned into the Building Society.

'We've got to stop her,' I said. 'She's probably doing a raid.'

It was the very worst of luck that, at that moment, I bumped into Mr Robertson from next door.

'Hey, hey, hey, young Damian,' he said, grabbing hold of my shoulders. 'What are you doing in town? Your mother said you were staying at home.'

I didn't know what to say.

'You'd better come with me,' he said. 'My wife will be worried silly, wondering where you are.'

I looked round at the would-be detectives.

'Sorry, guys. Something's turned up. I've got to go.'

Now we'd never find out about the blonde with the thin lips.

Chapter 5

When Mum came home, I could tell she'd had a tough day. She looked really stressed.

'I've had two calls on my mobile,' she said. 'One from Sue Greenspan who was collecting for charity outside the Post Office. And one from Elizabeth Travis at the library.'

She glared at me. 'Why were you running riot through the town this morning with a gang of hooligans? Knocking down old people. Wrecking the library. Can't I trust you for half a day, Damian?'

I hate it when she shouts. I try to understand. But it's hard on a kid who only needs a kind word and a plate of chips.

'Tomorrow,' she said, 'you're coming with me – like it or not. I'm catering at the local dog show and I'm not leaving you behind to get into more trouble. You can watch the dogs.'

Actually, I like dogs. So the dog show was cool.

I made quick phone calls to the kids who had come to the Detective School that morning.

'Be at the County Exhibition Hall by ten o'clock tomorrow for another training session,' I said. 'Bring a dog if you've got one.' (This was good thinking. No one would suspect kids with dogs were working as undercover trainee detectives.)

By the time I arrived with Mum, the dog show was in full swing.

I offered to help carry the food from the van. Mum's not all that fit at her age. But no. She wouldn't let me.

'I'll manage by myself, thank you, Damian,' she said. 'It's safer.'

So I left her to it and went and
settled into a ringside seat. Tod and
Lavender had already arrived with
their dog, Curly. Winston walked in
soon after with Thumper who smelled
really bad.

'Harry's coming later,' he said, 'but I
don't think the rest are keen to go
sleuthing on a Sunday.'

'Their loss,' I said. 'They'll never make the grade without the practice.'

At this point, Lavender started tugging at my sleeve in an agitated sort of way.

'Damian!' she said. 'I've theen her.'

'Seen who?'

'That blonde woman with the thin lipth. The one planning to wob the building thothiety.'

I took out my shades and put them on. At once, I was alert and ready for action. I looked round the hall, my eyes peeled.

'Over there!' said Lavender, waggling her finger. 'Thee's right in the middle of the ring! Look! Thee's the JUDGE!'

I could hardly believe it. The blonde was there all right and wearing a huge rosette. Here was my biggest chance yet to catch a crook red-handed. Not to mention the chance to prove my Criminal Theory number 3.

This is the plan I wrote.

Lavender, Winston and Harry to do:
Stay near the show ring
watch out for Mum if she comes
looking for me.

Me to do:
follow suspect when she leaves ring
take notes on criminal activities
contact Inspector Crockitt
talk to the Press and TV

Inspector Crockitt to do:
Arrest suspect
Put suspect in jail

We all sat and watched while the blonde woman judged the Small Dog competition. First she looked at one dog. Then the next. It took ages to check them all. I don't know why. It was obvious which was the best dog.

When she finally announced the winner, I was quite disgusted. The dog had hair right down to its feet and a stupid red bow on its head. It was owned by someone called Major Dalrymple. How would he like it if someone tied a bow in his hair (if he had any)?

She gave him a silver cup and a certificate and then she walked out of the ring.

'Right,' I said. 'I'm going to follow her. See what information I can get.'

I needed more hard facts if I was going to call the police and have her arrested.

'Take Curly with you,' said Lavender. 'Thee's a good guard dog. Dangerwoush teeth!'

I shrugged. I didn't need protection. I'm used to danger.

But Lavender insisted. 'You might get into a weally twicky thituation.'

Just to please Lavender, I did.

Outside the hall, I spotted the judge heading towards the refreshment room. The only snag was, Mum was in there, too.

I kept my wits sharp. I needed a disguise. There was a small changing room nearby and I found a large hat and a coat that fitted me, sort of. Not even my own mother would recognise me now.

I went into the refreshment room, tied Curly to the table leg and began to observe the blonde.

Activities of criminal blonde woman.
Puts 3 teaspoons of sugar in tea.
Drinks tea.
Opens bag
Takes roll of banknotes out of bag
and counts them!!!!!!!!!!!!!!!
Does this mean she did raid on
Building Society?
Probably!!!!!!!!!!!!!!

Just as I'd finished writing my notes, I saw Mum come out of the kitchen. She was carrying one of her chocolate gateaux. (My favourite.) It was too much for me. Even the best detectives need a break sometimes.

I decided that if I went up to the counter with my head well down, I could buy a slice and she'd never notice. But I forgot about Curly. She decided to follow me, dragging the table with her and wrapping her lead round a waiter's legs.

'Oy, you!' he said (very rudely, I thought). 'You can't bring dogs in here. You'll have to take him out.'

'It's a "her" actually,' I said.

At the sound of my voice, Mum looked up. 'Damian?' she said. 'What are you doing here? I told you to go and watch the show.'

'Sorry, Mum,' I said. 'I felt faint. I thought a piece of your gateau would make me feel better.'

She could have looked a bit more sympathetic but anyway, she cut a massive slice and put it on a paper plate.

'Go back to the show ring,' she said, 'and take that heap of hair with you.' (A mean way to describe Curly.)

'Righto, Mum,' I said and began to walk away with the gateau in one hand and Curly's lead in the other.

'And for goodness sake take off that ridiculous coat!' she called after me. She didn't realise I was in disguise. It's tough working undercover.

During all the fuss with Mum and the waiter, I had taken my eyes off the blonde. Big mistake. When I glanced over to her table, she was gone. Maybe she suspected that I was watching her. Maybe she'd made a run for it. Whatever – I wasn't going to let her get away.

Chapter 6

When I got back to the show ring Lavender amazed me once again with her powers of detection.

She looked at me and said, 'I thee you've been eating chocolate cake, Damian.'

How did she guess? The kid's a genius!

Unfortunately, I had to tell her that our suspect had given me the slip. 'Once they know you're on to them,' I said, 'things can get really tough.'

Lavender looked puzzled. 'But ithn't that her?' she said, pointing to the far side of the ring, behind the last row of seats. The suspect was standing there talking to someone.

'You've got laser eyes, you have,' said Harry.'

'Yeah!' said Winston. 'Well spotted, Lavender.'

'Brilliant,' said Tod.

No good getting too excited. There was real detective work still to be done – and I was going to do it.

'Right,' I said. 'I'm going to sneak over there.'

'But thee might thee you, Damian!' said Lavender.

'Cool it, Lavender. Nobody will see me. I can be almost invisible when I need to be. Watch and learn.'

Perfecting this skill had taken a lot of practice – in the kitchen, down the corridors at school, in the cinema. I had studied for months. Now was my chance to put it to use in preventing crime.

I dropped down flat onto the floor. Slowly, I moved forward keeping my body in contact with the ground, Commando fashion. It was not an easy exercise.

This took time but when I got round to the other side, the blonde was still there, talking to a man who looked familiar. Lucky or what? To get as close as possible, I hid under a seat in

the back row. Then I pressed my ear to
the ground and listened.

'. . . wasn't enough money . . .'

'The risk is too great . . .'

'. . . greedy . . .'

'. . . plan carefully . . .'

I couldn't hear every word for a very
good reason – Curly had followed me
and was stuffing her nose in my face. I
tried pushing her away but she started
whining and almost gave the game
away.

I might not have heard everything the blonde said but I heard enough. It was obvious that she was discussing the Building Society. I set off to go back with Curly in tow, to tell the others.

'They're planning a robbery,' I said as I sat down. 'And that man she's talking to – I've seen him before. I think he works at the Building Society.'

'Typical,' said Winston. 'He's in on it.'

I nodded wisely.

'Tho he'th a cwook, too!' said Lavender. 'You've got to do something to thtop them, Damian.'

She trusted me. I had to act fast.

'Lend me your mobile, Lavender,' I said. 'I'm going to ring Inspector Crockitt.'

Chapter 7

I left a message for the Inspector. It was perfectly clear.

'Come quick and arrest the judge at the Dog Show who is a dangerous bank robber.'

But the police can be very slow. A whole hour passed – and no one came.

Maybe the desk sergeant I spoke to hadn't written it down properly. Maybe he hadn't passed it on to Inspector Crockitt.

'Funny,' I said to the others. 'I thought he'd be here like a shot.'

'I don't think the police are coming,' said Harry. 'We're running out of time. The competition's nearly finished.'

Harry was right. The Large Dog competition was the last in the show. Our suspect was about to award the cup to the winner. Soon, I'd have to go home with Mum and another criminal would have escaped.

Suddenly, Winston stood up in his seat and pointed. 'Hey! Look who's got the cup,' he said. 'It's that major who won the other competition.'

Winston had obviously learned my
lessons about staying alert.

'That's not a major,' I said, staring
into the ring. 'He's the judge's partner
in crime. They're planning a robbery. I
heard them talking.'

'Cor!' said Winston. 'Then we've got
to act now. We can't wait for the
police.'

'What thall we do, Damian?'
Lavender asked.

I thought about it. Then I gave the
kids instructions – just simple things to
do. I would cope with the dangerous
stuff myself.

This is what happened.

I ran into the centre of the show ring. Hundreds of pairs of eyes were on me but I didn't care.

The judge (our suspect) looked horrified.

'Clear off!' she shouted. 'You're ruining the contest.'

But I refused to move. Instead, I turned to the people in the middle of the show ring standing with their dogs.

'This judge is a criminal,' I said. 'She's not fit to hand out cups. She's a thief.'

At that moment, the blonde bolted for the exit – and so did the major. It was just what I expected. But I was ready for them. I gave the signal to my trainee detectives and they released their dogs shouting, 'Go, go, go!' Then Curly and Thumper chased after the two crooks.

'Aaaahhhhgggg!' screamed the blonde and tripped over a loose piece of carpet.

'Noooooo!' yelled the major and tripped over the blonde.

'Woof, woof, woof!' barked the dogs and landed on top of them both.

The dogs in the competition joined in. Barking and yelping and jumping about. It was brilliant!

Security guards came shouting, 'Get those dogs off. They're dangerous!'

I stood there watching. Another
crime solved. Another crook punished.
But it didn't turn out exactly as I'd
planned. I suddenly found myself in
the grip of a burly security guard. I
was furious.

'What are you doing?' I demanded.
'Don't you know who I am?'

'You're the one that's caused this
riot,' he said.

I was shocked. 'But it's her you should be arresting,' I said, pointing to a leg sticking out from the pile of excited dogs.

The security guards didn't seem to know what to do. By the time Inspector Crockitt arrived, our chief suspect and the major were still stuck and calling for help. It was only when four police officers managed to pull the dogs off, that the criminals emerged, shaking and terrified.

'I confess. I confess,' said the judge.

Now this was what I wanted to hear.

The next day, there were big headlines in the local paper.

DAMIAN DOES IT AGAIN. DOG SHOW JUDGE HEADS FOR JAIL.

All the kids at school gathered round to read it.

'You're a bwilliant detective,' said Lavender.

'Yeah,' said Winston. 'Catching a bank robber like that.'

It was good to feel appreciated. But then Harry decided to read the article from start to finish. Every word.

'Wait a minute,' he said as he reached the bottom. 'It doesn't mention a bank robbery here. Or a building society, for that matter.'

I shrugged. 'So?'

'It says that the judge was being paid by the major for letting his dogs win.' He smirked and put down the paper. 'You were just lucky, Damian.'

Did it matter? I had solved a crime, hadn't I?

'If you athk me,' said Lavender, 'cheating at competitions is jutht as bad as wobbing banks. Don't you know that the major could thell puppieth for loths and loths of money if the pawents were pwize winners?'

Of course, I knew that. But I didn't say anything. I just nodded.

The following week, Inspector Crockitt called at school to talk about my part in solving the crime. He went on about not doing dangerous things and finding an adult when we're in trouble. All basic stuff really. I'd heard it loads of times.

Before he left, the Inspector wanted to have a quiet word with me. (He likes to pick up tips on how to solve crimes.) But today I could only suggest he speeded up his response time.

'You got to the dog show ages after I left the message for you,' I said.

'Sorry, Damian,' he replied. 'I thought it was a joke.'

'A joke?'

'Yes, I wasn't sure the message was from you.'

I nearly choked. Is this the way to run a police force?

I have now thought of how to avoid mistakes like this in future. I have written to Inspector Crockitt outlining my idea for a secret code. It will be known only to the two of us. I can send messages as often as I like with tip-offs about suspected criminals. It's a brilliant idea and I think he'll be dead pleased.

I'm just waiting for a reply.

DAMIAN DROOTH
SUPERSLEUTH

SPYCATCHER

by Barbara Mitchelhill
with illustrations by Tony Ross

Lavender is very
upset. Her friendly
neighbour has become
very grumpy because he thinks
his inventions are being
stolen. Damian agrees to
investigate, and where
better to start than the
meeting of Young
Inventors? Using his
special skills, he
soon uncovers a
spy – but has he
got the right
man?

9781842705674 £3.99

DAMIAN DROOTH
SUPERSLEUTH

SERIOUS GRAFFITI

by Barbara Mitchelhill
with illustrations by Tony Ross

When the Headmaster
tells everyone off about
graffiti in one of the
school toilets, Damian decides
to act. Luckily he has lots of
willing detective
apprentices. What with
sorting out a handwriting
test, and looking for
matching paint, he
needs all the help he
can get! But even
Damian isn't
expecting to be
accused of the
crime himself!

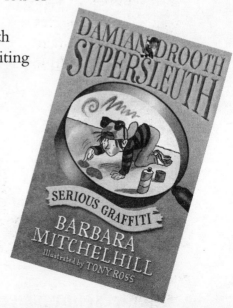

9781842706503 £3.99

DAMIAN DROOTH
SUPERSLEUTH

Do you think Damian Drooth is an ace detective? Would you like to find out more about him? Then check out the Damian Drooth website!

You'll find puzzles, screensavers, door hangers — and lots, lots more!

www.andersenpress.co.uk/damiandrooth